I0725975

LANDMARKS

microfiction and prose poems

edited by

Cassandra Atherton

SPINELESS WONDERS

www.shortaustralianstories.com.au

Spineless Wonders

PO Box 220

STRAWBERRY HILLS

New South Wales, Australia, 2012

shortaustralianstories.com.au

First published by Spineless Wonders 2017

Text copyright © remains with individual authors.

Cover image and design by Richard Holt

Editorial assistance by Taliesyn Gottlieb. Layout by Bronwyn Mehan.

Typeset in Franklin Gothic Book

Printed and bound by Lightning Source Australia

ISBN 978-1-925052-31-2

Catalogue-in-print

A823.4

Landmarks prose poems and microfiction/

Atherton, Cassandra (ed)

LANDMARKS

microfiction and prose poems

This project has been assisted by the Australian Government through the Australia Council, its arts funding and advisory body.

'Books, like landscapes, leave their marks in us. (...) Certain books, though, like certain landscapes, stay with us even when we left them, changing not just our weathers but our climates.'
 – Robert Macfarlane, *Landmarks*

Contents

BIOGRAPHIES

EDITOR

THE JOANNE BURNS AWARD

ABOUT JOANNE BURNS

Introduction

Emily Dickinson wrote: 'If you take care of the small things, the big things take care of themselves. You can gain more control over your life by paying closer attention to the little things.' Microliterature may appear unassuming on the page, taking up very little space and using fewer words than even short stories, but as a form, it opens out to embrace things bigger than itself. In this way, the small things in microliterature provide the foundation for the entire structure of the narrative. Dickinson scholar, Paul Hetherington best describes this when he argues that prose poems are 'TARDIS-like' in the way they 'reveal more than their actual size on the page would appear to allow'[1]. The TARDIS is famous for being bigger on the inside – the interior much larger than its exterior – and when used as a metaphor for microliterature, it demonstrates the way the short form subverts its visual cues by becoming larger as the reader wanders into the narrative.

Indeed, the microliterature in this anthology tackles the theme of Landmarks: critical or celebratory, watershed moments or turning points in history, culture, or in relationships. It encourages thinking about literal landmarks and marks on the land(scape). In this way, this anthology could almost be viewed as an oxymoron: something small – 200 words or less – taking on a prominent feature, spectacle or marker as its narrative concern. However, far from setting up the writer for failure, it has resulted in rich and textured narratives that work with spaces and metaphors in unique and memorable ways.

The microliterature here ranges across most short forms of writing: flash fiction, prose poetry, postcard fiction and nonfiction vignettes. Given the richness of form, the anthology has been arranged as a series of juxtaposed micro-flights. Instead of placing all the flash fiction together, all the light-hearted pieces together or all the pieces with historical landmarks together, the microliterature in this collection has been grouped in small numbers with a focus on colligation. In this way, the writing in this anthology traverses subject matter from droughts, hunters, caring for elderly mothers and the burning of the Aboriginal flag, to birthmarks, arms and even the desire to be Amelie. In this anthology the little things are coruscating moments that lead to a variety of weighty awakenings.

Congratulations to those shortlisted for the Newcastle Writers Festival/Joanne burns Microlit award and to all of the writers who entered the competition. It was a difficult process shortlisting entries as the standard was incredibly high and the subject matter expansive. The two winning pieces are Tim Heffernan's 'Barunga Conversation' and Dael Allison's 'Breakwall' (Newcastle). These beautifully crafted pieces of microlit are memorable for their unique approach to the theme and for their brilliant control in this short form.

Thank you to Rosemarie Milsom, director of the Newcastle Writers Festival and judges Joanna Atherfold Finn and Karen Whitelaw for their incredible work in extending this award to the Newcastle Writers Festival.

Thank you to the commissioned writers: Evelyn Araluen, Julie Chevalier, Shady Cosgrove, Tricia Dearborn, Paul Hetherington, Bella Li, Susan Midalia, Sam Wagan Watson, Patrick West, Chloe Wilson and Danielle Wood for their wonderful pieces of microfiction and prose poetry.

Thank you to Taliesyn Gottlieb for her editorial assistance and to Richard Holt for his gorgeous cover design and his quirky and memorable piece in this anthology. Thank you to joanne burns, who lends her name to this award and is a pioneer in Australia for the short form. Finally, thank you to Spineless Wonders' publisher, Bronwyn Mehan, for providing an incredible opportunity for writers to have their work published in beautiful, intelligent, enduring books.

Cassandra Atherton, 2016

1. 'Unconscionable mystification'?: rooms, spaces and the prose poem', *New Writing: The International Journal for the Practice and Theory of Creative Writing*, 12 (3), pp265 – 281.

Tim Heffernan

BARUNGA CONVERSATION

cross-legged he squats demonstrating his empathy, under-
standing and handiwork. an old fella speaks, 'draughty shelter
this,' as sad eyes roam over a corrugated landscape. the
compact white leader shifts his weight, 'a true reconciliation is
in this draft treaty.' an empty promise's silence disperses the
floating words. wind on a windless day. 'listen mate. negotiations
in accordance with constitutional processes will lead to commit-
tees responsible for consultation, organisation and dialogue that
will culminate in expected conclusions allowing for a more self
determined management with compensation for dispossession
and in addition a recognition of integral national systems.' the
old fella replies, 'big words. long sentence.'

Dael Allison

BREAKWALL

Why don't they do this in summer, she mutters, clambering down the rocks to where he stands. No fishing-line and no bucket, just staring into the grey waves which crash at his feet, then succumb to the tide's outgoing rush. She finds a flat surface and settles, buttoning her jacket. 'Always treacherous, Newcastle Harbour,' she says, raising her voice to counter the wind.

Some tell her straight-up to piss off. Not this one. Shoulders hunched, arms clenched across his chest, he won't engage. She starts talking about the wrecks, over two hundred on Nobbys, around Stockton, down the coast. 'Lovely boats, splintered apart. The *Caroline*, *Yarra Yarra*, *Cumberland*, all lives lost, and *Bluebell*, a ferry, took three women down.'

'The *Cawarra* was the worst,' she adds thoughtfully. 'Sixty people thrown into terrible seas. No hope. Body parts washed up for weeks: legs, arms, unrecognizable heads.'

Suddenly he's gone. She watches him scramble up the rocks. From the concrete path he glares down, gives her the third finger. Then he is running, back towards town.

Cold makes her joints congeal. She tugs her jacket closer. It's new, from the op-shop, and red's a good colour for a grey day.

Evelyn Araluen

MUSEUM

I discovered a Kunstkabinett on the third floor filled with the boxed and framed dead. You were the one who told me what that word meant, a cabinet of curiosities, a wonder room of natural and unnatural history. Inside I met a loris with a toothache who helped me unpin the butterflies from their display. They fluttered between the tree trunk ghosts of a rainforest, and dragged their feet across the frozen nectar of ashen floristry. I asked the loris if he remembered you, and he asked me to describe your teeth. I told him of your crooked lateral incisors and of the way my chest feels when I think of you too much. What is here is not here, he tells me, is label and diagram and formaldehyde. Surrounded by moths and monarchs uncrucified we begin unbaying the botany. I do not know who they are, the scientists, the ethnographers, the mapmakers, but here we tip out a landscape of their spoils. Sawdust spills from the bellies of birds and the turtle howls with hollow. We tear the charts from the window, we are lattice lit explorers, and we are drenched in dust and gesture. The butter-flies splutter against water, against glass.

Sam Wagan Watson

ANVIL AND PUNCH

i Anvil

How I should ever stop feeling regret for the *great* poem commenced + never finished. That's the price I pay for entering into an agreement with a page + not really committing to my end of the bargain. There doesn't necessarily need to be a happy ending for every composition, but an unfinished + abandoned page contains the saddest conclusion of them all...

I hammer, I hammer, I hammer myself raw...

ii. Punch-line

Sometimes it hurts more than having a heart broken by someone I truly love because an unfinished poem hasn't been mused over or appreciated by a raw audience, + knowing what I know: what we could have had, could have shared in creative affinity. There are life-long sentences that refuse to audibly speak back to me...but sometimes as I flick through a journal they tend to make idle threats...

If you don't finish me...I shall have to finish you!

Danielle Wood

HARE

She is not the tortoise in that tale. Though erratic, fretful bursts of speed have served her well enough, in truth she is only a moderate success. She comforts herself that real life has no finish line.

It's New Year's Day and resolve hangs in the air alongside the tinderbox threat of bushfire. Circling the home paddock on the mower, she watches the falling shafts of grass, thistle, caltrop, boneseed. Then: look! A hare! A wire-sprung twist of fur and fright, zig-zagging for the fence line!

Left behind, in full view of the hawkish sky: a leveret.

Slow by steady milky drop, it grows, and she is proud. It licks her with a lizard-blue tongue, lets her stroke its fur-slippered feet, dances figure eights between her ankles.

But February brings instinct, March fear. Now her footfall is enough to set its heart off like a firecracker. The young animal slams into windows, walls.

You can't let it go, says a friend who knows all about vermin.

About the right size for jugging, her husband says.

Putting it in the rabbit-proof garden is only a half-decision. On the second day she comes home to a thistledown drift of fur, a glimpse of the wrong side of skin, the bright glint of new bone.

How she cries.

Chloe Wilson

ARM'S LENGTH

They said *keep that boy at arm's length*. But whose arm? The arm of an orangutan, or a tyrannosaurus rex? A rat's arm? A baby's arm? A spider's arm - and if so, which one of the eight should she measure? *Your arm*, they said. So she took a saw and severed her arm at the shoulder. When they said *you still have your other arm*, she offered them the saw, and said: Here. Go ahead. Later, they planted the arms in the earth. No-one was surprised when they sprouted roots which found each other underground.

Samantha See

PERPETUAL MOTION

Moving to a big city was by far the ballsiest thing I had ever done in my life. Ten times ballsier than that time I ate three week old Chinese out of the communal fridge at uni. I remember thinking that I no longer had anything that tied me to any place anymore, thinking that my internal compass was shot, that I would feel lost forever. I tried to grip onto anything that I thought could become an anchor. First it was this b-grade dumpling shop that had a blinking neon sign and do you want to know it shut down due to a health and safety violation within a month of my first visit. Again and again I was denied my right for mooring until one night I was washing the dishes, looking out my apartment window, and I saw this star that seemed to be bigger and brighter than any other and I thought once and for all that it was my anchor. Turns out that it was the 1020 flight from Dubai, but that made me realise we are all fluid, we are all perpetual, we are all our own landmark. We shine brighter when we are moving.

Paul Hetherington

JUT

Falls of fruit in the garden, and morning's triangular shadow, catching the house. Yachts like postage stamps on a blue envelope; your gestures smoothing them. We walked where dogs barked in kennels and along a curving drive. "There," you pointed, taking in the west side of the bay. "My ancestors owned it all." "And the people before them?" "Gone before we arrived. A few graves were found." That day I gathered driftwood large as a shinbone. Air shimmied; I needed to sit. You pointed out a landmark you adored. "That jut of cliff, and the stream that lets itself gently and softly down."

Barnaby Smith

TIME/TRIAL

Under this tree that bird was murdered, circa 1989, an infant's play for a baptism in domination. Time to do this, swap your face for its face, time to exist here; remaining, trigger species memory for a portal to conduct the task. Injured already, she flops through the trees to this one tree where we corner her – memory making her feminine – with mushy plywood, truly gents on a mission in the overcast minutes before the prime time line-up. She is cornered against that foreign shrub and heroically squished under planks. Cartilage, feathers, beak and chirp with mud engorged – two noble births lending their weight to the crushing wood. Small grey bubble bulges from a plywood corner, lung or ventricle or something, under here is a ground-up eyeball that will passively inspect your patterns from the vantage point of these roots through each turning point and abode. She meets you here now, with lots of other birds and the afternoon feels the same though we were gallant then. A glistening internal organ hangs low and keeps time, erasing the pout that came with small triumphs... a strimmer should suffice for this area. Here, you try.

Tenzin Bereny

BEFORE AND AFTER

You notice her gaze keeps slipping to the counter as she takes your order. Your eyes only touch in tiny moments, but know what you're seeing; the hint of worries that don't sleep. Since the yolk and white of your mind became scrambled eggs you've been seeing it in others. That gooey yellow brain on your dry morning toast. You'd bet anything she eats the same breakfast.
She's drug-use thin with heavily freckled skin. She's wearing smoky eyes that don't hide the tired. As she passes your debit card back, you read the tattoo on her arm.
'Nothing to fear.'
Instead of trying conversation you slump into an olive green armchair in the corner of the café. She mops the floors with bad posture and you wonder about the world she carries on her back. Somehow she's still walking. So are you?
You want to grab her hand, throw a dart at the faux vintage map on the wall and walk – run – fly together to wherever it lands.
If you found another page in the atlas, would you have an A.D.?
Or, will you both carry your zero years forever?

Harriet McInerney

THE CITY WAS GROWING INSIDE HER

She felt it first when she moved into the apartment. On the top floor, the neighbours were friendly and the view spanned many rooftops. On tiptoes she could just glimpse the ocean.

Inside her mouth was cramped and busy. She peered at her reflection. Her parted lips were bright red. Her teeth were swollen. And buildings spiralled upwards from each of her molars, lower canines were terraces, first premolar an uncomfortable cathedral. In the wet space under her tongue, the city converged in a soupy sprawl.

As the city grew it was harder for her to speak. She slurred sounds. The neighbours invited her round for dinner, and she said *shanksh sho mush, I'd ove oo.* She told them of her years living alone in desolate coastal towns, but wasn't sure if it was how she said it, or what she said, that shocked them.

Later, full bellied, she felt the calcified buildings expand to the edges of her mouth. It made her feel tired. When she woke the next day she wanted to stand on her tiptoes and see the ocean, but she didn't have the energy. In the city, life remained busy.

Marjorie Lewis-Jones

THE SHAPE YOU MAKE

Some cold trail she's been following. Chilled scent. Led her to the wood. Led her to the edge. Some dead bird. Taken apart by teeth. Some feathers spread on the hot ground. Scattered. Small smears of red. Tendons and tissue. Sinews and muscle. This is what climbs. Vessel of the mind. There's a bottle. Cloudy. Gripe water. A lagoon of sky. Rope sags under. Umbilical cord to boat. Never tried. This is how it was and ever will be. Empty. The shape you make. Cupped on a surface. Crib. Cradle. Ceremony. Little coffin. Very light.

Danielle Baldock

THE TURNING

The air conditioning in hotels is always too cold. She can't tell if she is shivering from the icy blasts from the angled vents above the bed, or from the unassailable truth that they'll never be together again. The lights of passing cars flick endlessly across the not-quite-closed navy curtains, and she tries to muffle her ragged breathing in the dark so he won't ask her again if she's okay.

Ahead of them they still have the morning to face, the muzak in the glass lift, the cheery waiters, trying not to catch each other's eyes. She will clutch the tepid coffee with trembling fingers, her fingernails clicking on the thick white cup, studying the creases in the white tablecloth, and the way the swirling pattern in the carpet doesn't quite match up in the corners. She will feel him looking at her, so she will look intently at the blurry words of the newspaper.

And then there will be the long drive home, past the hills and the lake, through silence and traffic, to their separate lives.

But for now, the dark is thick, and she presses her hands over her face to keep herself in.

Gavin Austin

MY MOTHER'S SONG

'Not too hot, Mum?' I ask.

My mother's skin is pale; wrinkled like an old sheet from the laundry basket. Her white flesh marbled with blue veins, wilting breasts rest on her belly. The water rushes over her, pooling at the base of her spine where shapeless buttocks meet the plastic stool.

'We're going out,' I say.

'Ah,' she manages. She folds her hands on her lap, leans forward, hiding them as if to keep them safe.

Suddenly I've become a stranger in the room.

I ask Mum to stand. Her knuckles whiten on the shower handrail as I begin to pat her down with a towel. Steadily, I move her to the bedroom chair where she collapses, exhausted.

The nurses tell me her days are spent quietly sitting, or shuffling the corridors looking for her handbag, her bed ... something.

I choose slacks and a jumper, having managed her into undergarments without much fuss. Feeding her stick-arms into the sleeves, she stares at me with clouded blue eyes. Death seems to be taking its time playing out her song – note by note – words are the first to go. How much of her remains?

Maree Gallop

LOST IN TRANSLATION

James speaks with an accent of adventure. Sometimes the stormy seas of uncharted waters roll from his mouth. Other times he exhales exotic tropical air. But lately I've heard the dusky sound of an imminent shipwreck.

'Madd. Hurry up!'

James swigs the remaining water from our drink bottle, readjusts his backpack and powers off toward the Breadknife. My throat's parched and the blister on my left heel rubs against my new hiking boot. I sit down amid the Wurrumbungles on a fallen eucalypt and think of Tom.

Tom speaks with an accent of wisdom. He pauses between words, breathes in the eucalypt air and transforms it into an ancient story, earthy and rich.

I haven't told James that Tom and I honeymooned here, at the Warrumbungles. I was afraid to. At the mere mention of Tom's name, lava flows from James's mouth like the volcano that formed the crooked mountains surrounding us.

Overtime, I misinterpreted Tom's accent as boring, so still and silent as if he were the rocks and the starlit sky. Now, it reverberates through me like the echo of my name that went on and on and on as he sang it to the valley.

'Madeline ...line...line'.

Mark O'Flynn

FRAGMENT FROM A WESTERN

... when the horse fell and the rider fell the dust caught them with a tenderness beyond the normal capacity of dust to feel, its race was finished. The horse would never run again. In a better life it had a paddock full of lupins to look forward to, a gentle incline up which to gallop, oats in the feedbag, a sandy track to the top of One Tree Hill where, given a favourable wind, the Church bells might be heard – bang bang bang – calling the pious to prayer. The rider hawked and spat: stupid, useless, decrepit old gluepot, bag of bones, get up, fit for nothing but the dog food factory. The landmark of his hat in the dust. He cared not how far the spavined nag had carried him only that it had failed now, the posse hot on his tail, the wasps of bullets buzzing past his ears. The sheriff gaining ground, bent low in the saddle. The horse heaved a mighty sigh, its load spilled, lather slick on its flanks from the chase. It had given its best. It just needed a minute more... a minute... The dust, the grass, the wasps ...

Mark Roberts

YARANIGH'S GRAVE

Molong NSW

Thomas Mitchell accompanies Yaranigh on a walk through the land of the Wailwan people

Mitchell wants to follow rivers. He doesn't know country so he takes horses, bullocks boats & food. He walks slow with so much stuff. 8 drays, drawn by 80 bullocks; 2 boats; 13 horses; 3 light carts, 250 sheep, constituting the chief part of the animal food. The rest consists of gelatine, and a small quantity of pork. I take him away from bora grounds and avoid good hunting areas. I say 'he is passing through he will not stay. He will not find what he is looking for'.

Richard Holt

OBLONG

I was destined to write. It was Beggs who saw it first. 7D. Ah, Thompson, he said. Always the wordsmith. Yes, Sir, I said – not my finest line but the pressure was on. Perhaps, as you enjoy writing so much, I might set you a task...what do you say? Yes Sir, I said. I must say I'm impressed, he said. It's not every day one is offered such an opportunity – a chance to create something lasting. Many might have resorted to the visual. But you've captured the very essence in written language. Bard-like... brilliant. Do you think, I said, warming to his response. I do, he said. He took another look at my creation. Yes, certainly. Incredible. Come with me, he said. Leading me by the earlobe he trudged me back to the classroom, muttering, all the while, extraordinary...quite extraordinary. Beggs showed me the possibilities. I had only dabbled. He opened my eyes. The whole board, Sir? Yes, Thompson, the whole board. Did he think the challenge would defeat me? Instead I found in it the true potential of the form. Concrete poetry – the board a solid block of letters. I will not write penis in the new footpath. I will not write penis in the new footpath. Over and over. I will not write penis. I will not write penis. The meter precise. The rhythm like heartbeats. I will not...

Jen Saunders

INFINITY LOOPS

Spinner said he'd meet me at Hendo's because he had to get the money out. So I went round past the Entertainment Centre. I didn't like being at Hendo's by myself so I took my time. Hendo's twitchy. Could never be sure what sort of weird shit he'd come out with. Alien abductions, conspiracies. Spinner knew how to stir him up without making him pissed off, so we'd get a laugh as well as a couple of free cones.

I rolled past the big locked doors of the Centre. Posters for opera and ballet and wrestling. Never been in before. Thought I might go see the wrestling one day. Take Spinner.

I waved to the cleaner inside. Because it was Sunday it was just me and her. No security lads. She gave me a little flick-wave but no smile. Another skatie-hater.

I swung round the three giant flagpoles in clean infinity loops, my wheels nice and loud. Spinner's gran was still pissed off about the day the Mayor burned the Aboriginal flag, right there.

'I stayed up all night sewing that flag! By hand!' she'd say. All that was long before me and Spinner were born. But she didn't forget.

Patrick West

IN BRIEF

One morning, a story appears in the 'In Brief' column of the newspaper that is published every day except Sundays. The subheading reads, like a chapter title from a children's book of mysteries, 'The First Ocean'. An African source reports that a young man has begun (to coin a phrase) 'the swim of a lifetime to Australia.'

The item is positioned about as close to the middle of the news-sheet as it is possible to get, before the reading eye might disappear, and drown into itself, beneath the many folds of print-barnacled paper gathered into a thickness at the central seam: an interminglement of words, and of black-and-white pictures like B&W TV.

There is no satisfactory explanation given for the unusual subheading. There can be no happy sequel to the few lines of this story.

Still, they'd gathered at the shore, these men, stroking their chins as the sun rose, their faces sour and grumpy. They might still have been tucked up in bed, contrary as they liked beneath the counterpane, were it not for the doubt whispered into several ears simultaneously, as midnight stirred the sleeping world, that this would be something more than the sort of swim you embark on, only to wash the sleep from your eyes.

Rebecca Lehman

ONE DAY

Right now it's just a field. Nothing special, yellow grass and barb wire fences, like a million other fields across the land. Right now it's just a field for cattle.

One day soon it will be quick sale for some fast cash. Then the field will become a lot, in the middle of which a tech company will build a concrete square. For a while it will be used to test rockets. There will be a few caravans scattered around, but it will still just be a lot. As the company grows, the lot will become a base. Caravans will be replaced with buildings, and those rockets will become the way in which satellites reach orbit. The base will grow bigger and become a complex, with multi-story buildings and large steel hangars. People will come from around the world. Scientists will study, engineers will build, children will learn, and visitors will watch the rockets take flight. One day, far in the future, this will be the launch pad of the Mars colonists. A testament to their bravery, this place will be a monument to the greatest adventure mankind will ever undertake...

But right now, it's just a field.

Susan Midalia

THE BRIGHT SILVER
PIN

A prize-winning, best-selling and internationally acclaimed writer once pronounced, to general approbation, that 'if a novel was a map of a country, a short story was the bright silver pin that marked the crossroads.' Another writer who'd never won a prize or sold a single copy of his only short story collection, had never received any form of approbation, whether general, colonel or sergeant, and who had always considered narrative (both the longer and shorter forms) to be an unequivocally temporal mode, pondered and puzzled over the use of those spatial metaphors by the prize-winning, best-selling etc etc writer. Did the 'the bright silver pin' refer to a stylistic and structural landmark, a means of illuminating our crucial psychological, moral and existential choices in life? And did the writerly act of using said pin presuppose that our life-in-time was essentially comprised of turning-points, crises, epiphanies? In which case, those spatial metaphors were indeed misplaced, since they did not escape the inescapable temporality of our miserable life-in-time. And on re-reading what he had just written, hadn't he, the non-prize-winning etc etc writer, used a tautology in the preceding sentence? Or was it a redundancy?

Self-editing had never been his strong point.

Emma Ashmere

AFTER THE STORM

Headlights flash across my mother's beehive and my father's towelling hat. She stops knitting. He's talking about UFOs again, how they tailed his Wirraway over New Guinea during the war.

We drive all night, sleep all day, wake to egg and bacon pie, grey paddocks, yellow hills, dry creeks, stop-watch timed pisses, dogs on tuckerboxes, pink salt lakes, until we reach my stranger cousins' house on stilts swaying over leech-laced ferns, a jungle world of pointed mountains and pillared clouds, where birds walk and foxes fly.

I lie in a bunk squinting at the swollen stars hanging close. Frogs croak. Geckoes skitter. Spiders embroider mosquito nets as my father and uncle drink the night.

That first morning I float in a soupy swimming pool. A flash of light in the green-black sky.

'Look, dad. They've followed us.'

'Get inside,' my uncle shouts.

And when the storm has passed and my mother and uncle are sweeping up the broken glass, and my cousins are making snowmen with piles of steaming hail, I wade after my father through the shredded trees towards the sunken shimmer of the tennis court.

I watched the sky as he knelt and wept.

Elizabeth
Tyson-Doneley

PAPER LINING

It's getting late. The TV show I was watching has just finished. I'm in the kitchen toasting muffins, spreading them with butter. The rain falls light and fresh, making me crave a cup of tea. I lean against the bench and eat, while my cat licks at her bowl, her long hair speckled with drops of water. She is like a little adventurer come in from the mountains, searching for a warm place to sleep. I bend down and gently scratch behind her ears. It's my first time living alone. I remember the landlord telling me about an old woman who lived here before me, also with a cat, until she passed away. The paper she put down in the cupboards and drawers is still there. I'm greeted by the scent of it when I go to get my cup.

Janet Thomas

UNDERPASS

On the tiled veranda with its deep set, screened windows are Nonna, Nonno and a boy. She can see them from the bus, forced because of roadworks and warm summer rain to inch past the house. The boy and his grandfather sit next to each other on a cane lounge. To the east, where the uncivil arms of three cranes eclipse the humbled sun, the neighbours' house once shielded them from the main road. Even its rubble has gone, taken for landfill.

The boy knows nothing of the neighbours, of shared weekends bottling tomatoes stored like hope at the back of kitchen cupboards, of cherries preserved in grappa hidden like memories at the bottom of the wardrobe beneath the suit Nonno wore to his children's weddings.

Nonna speaks to the boy. He nods, she reaches out to touch his head but he curls into his grandfather's side. The grandfather stirs cereal in a bowl, spoons it into the boy's mouth. The bus shifts gear and rolls onward; the old woman limps into the house and is swallowed by the screen door. A cyclist speeds past house, bus and the nascent shape of a four lane underpass.

Susi Fox

ROAD TO GUNDAGAI

joey is high on china white in the back of the vee dub when i pull up at the dog on the tuckerbox. we're half-way through our grand tour of austraya. joey said he was wantin to make a mockumentary of austraya's big things but i think he just wanted to scout medical clinics, pitchin his supposed rotten, broken spine for some more patches of junk.

the dog is tiny, i say. what a crappy, metal thing. it is sittin on a tuckerbox though.

baby, this shit's strong, joey says.

you should see its face, i say, lookin up at the stars like the foods just gunna drop from the sky.

joey starts moanin, blissin out in the back.

that dog's sure gunna be waitin a long time. his owner ain't returnin any time soon. No sir-ree.

joey don't say nothin from the back.

joey?

i jump over the leather seat to smack his cheeks, thump his chest, blow air down his throat. at least he's smiling, a big, chilled out smile on his blue lips, which is more than i can say for that damn dog on that fuckin box who ain't botherin to smile back at all.

Jodi Vial

THE SPAN

Only the river remembers how it felt to be without the bridge. Its heavy feet dig into the rock and its metal uprights stencil shadows on the water. The day it filled the sky, the bridge became a beacon for boys who had forgotten their way across the river and only wanted to fly. In a timeless procession they leap, hands outstretched, into their fate and future. The river remembers one boy who flew into dark water and stayed with her for the longest time. She holds this memory where she once held him – down among her sun-starved, slimy stones, where only water dares to journey and that never ends. Many cross her now but she does not feel them and they do not feel her. They do not know, as the river does, that in the span of a life you can leave a mark on the land or you can let it leave a mark on you.

Karen Manton

SHOT TOWER

The old, red brick shot tower rises with sentinel dignity into the blue, wisps of white cloud dare to smudge the sky, while below, the freeway gushes a river of wheeled metal and fume. The tall onlooker watches through eye windows, arches in the red brick. Are there stairs inside? – I used to wonder – spiralling upward, becoming so narrow only a child could fit. There was no smoke for this tower that looks like a chimney, it was height they wanted, to drop their lead spheres and make them perfect on the way down. I used to stare at this monument while we inched along the road.

'Keep the windows up,' my mother would say, 'or we'll asphyxiate.'

A bird battles against the wind above the highest point.

'It is the tallest shot tower,' my mother asks me to remember the fact.

I wonder on all the empty silos, empty chimneys, empty shot towers, how they gape. We leave them to hold their shadows, and house the pigeons. While for years, decades, a lifetime, we pass the tall presence, the sundial of our days that casts a shadow over the cemetery, the cracked ground we trust.

Richenda Rudman

LEAVING

We packed the lives of Marlene, Trevor and six of Marlene's children into rock sample boxes Roy got from his job as a geologist's assistant.

Junk, like split plastic ashtrays and stubby holders from The Palace Hotel, and a stained mauve silk bag with Marlene's kids' baby teeth were sealed into the cardboard boxes.

'Youse better not have pinched anything!' said Marlene, who sat and watched.

Marlene had taken Catherine's week-old baby from one of the stuck-together flats we all lived in at 55 Hanbury Street. She'd taken him home to cuddle and re-live womb-filling and suckling. Catherine woke to an empty bassinet and the sound of the mother-scream from her guts.

Catherine's husband, back from the mine, gave them an ultimatum: be gone by Saturday or I go to the police. Trevor – not his real name – said they'd leave.

Three trips for boxes and people in our shaking Holden panel van to the bus. We followed it out of town, past piles of beer cans in the red dirt that marked a tinny's worth of distance from Kalgoorlie to Perth.

And past dried wreaths nailed to white trunks of scrubby trees.

Jennifer Porter

OCHRE

She finds a patch of warm red dirt a couple of metres from the cliff edge, protected from the breeze by a melaleuca and a large boulder, her boulder. She stoops to light the joint before stretching her legs out on the silty ground and leaning back against the rock. The baked earth feels like someone's lap, some long buried memory of being held.

Her cheekbone still hurts when she smiles, or squints. She'd thought he was past all that. Hadn't he done some compulsory course while he was inside? She shuffles over and pulls the dress out of the hollow at the edge of the rock. It's started to turn from ivory to earth-coloured, ochre. She brings the cool taffeta up to her face, breathes in the scent of Red Door, then rests it against her cheek, like some ancient poultice.

The flames dance across the dress like a restless spirit trapped too long. They tumble and spread until she's sitting in a horse-shoe of fire. The grasses sizzle and pop in the heat before the melaleuca lights up, a twiggy effigy. She stands to meet its fiery eye before turning toward the cool green of the ocean.

Hilary Hewitt

DROUGHT

Blossom frilled like a childhood dress, a few bulbs that grow wild by the broken drainpipe – these have survived. You take rusting red scissors and fill a glass jar. One iris, pale as this early spring sky; cut from the neighbour's side of the fence, but who's counting now?

The ward is quiet. Bags hang from the drip-stand, their tubes carry fluids; her mouth is wide open and dry. You hold the flowers close, whisper the names you learned as a child. The narcissus are wet, they carry the memory of clouds. She opens one milky eye.

Amanda Berry

AS WE THAT ARE LEFT

As the beam of light passed over the stone, we stood silently, remembering. Greater Love Hath No Man etched permanently into the floor under the central pyramid. The assembled crowd dissipated into the sanctuary. Without intention, we'd crossed the blade-perfect grass into this Classical temple.

For most of the flawless afternoon we'd strolled through gardens, observing and observed, in a real-life Impressionist landscape full of people pushing prams, dog-walking, picnicking... and a couple, seduced into punting on the Ornamental Lake. Warmth was only in the light; icy shadows were claiming the high ground when we climbed the stairs.

'Have you been here before?' I said.

'No, never,' he replied.

Looking down from the promenade, the olive tree glinted golden and luminous. In the interest of peace, I said nothing more.

His private war had been devastating, obliterating and bloody on a cellular level. Unseen explosions: a miniscule atrocity. Severing. Erasing. Scrambling memory and tangling logic. The greatest casualty was the present.

Later I'd find pixelated proof that we had been here, only a few years before. For now, I reached for his hand. Together, we left the Forgotten Shrine and walked towards the city lights and the low-slung, winter moon.

Shady Cosgrove

SANCTUARY

The fridge followed her home and sat on the doorstep. It was a vintage model with rounded edges and one door, the freezer tucked inside. Her husband said it would have to go or be put to use. It blocked the entryway – anyone coming or leaving had to squeeze around it: an awkward negotiation, no question. She asked around the neighbourhood. She took a photo and made copies. Found: one loving, used, food-cooling unit. No takers. It waited patiently – always empty, beautifully clean. Then the washing machine turned up. This was spick, 1600 rpms and front-end loading. Not that it mattered, parked out on the concrete driveway with no hook-up. In the evenings, she'd lean against its white metal and watch the fridge – the air crisp with the smell of wet grass, a belt of stars overhead. She began staying outside later and later until she woke one morning, her neck sore. A blender and vacuum cleaner had appeared, leaning against the fridge. And beyond, the lawn was packed with dryers and deep freezers, ovens and dishwashers, all of them perched like giant metal birds.

Lisa Reily

MUM'S GARDEN

Vanilla sandstone stolen from a local park. A fake nail, snapped in the heist, is shaken from my mother's gardening glove onto our thick, green lawn. And a miniature Stonehenge takes shape around our new above-ground pool.

My small hands are scratched white by the sugared stone, but it's worth it. I rest a blistered palm in the promising water as it fills. We have our own pool – Clark Rubber blue stretched over sand – and a new rockery...

We are back at the park again. Shaded by paperbarks, we collect chunks of rock and pretty river stones. Mum concretes them into our lives. And by morning, a 'dog pond'.

I step out to our yard; a phallic stack of river stones towers into the sky. Our dog paddles reluctantly around it; a spectacle as the stack chugs and spurts – a 'dog fountain' – due to Mum's clever garden hose engineering.

Our ingenious fake rock, strategically placed, hides our spare key. Concealed in the strawberry patch, jam jars of rolled up money Mum won at the races. And under the fallen leaves of Mum's favourite tree, beneath her blue violets, a lifetime of dogs loved; wrapped and buried in their blankets.

Tess Pearson

FLY IN FLY OUT

Fly in. His view through the aircraft window is framed by bitter-sweet goodbyes. Blur of heat waves over asphalt, yellow lines, acceleration, dry mouth, g-force, lift, and then… Buoyancy. His small world shrinks into the wider aerial landscape. When they come into view, the gentle paleness of the saltpans reminds him of his older sister's chicken pox scars: whispery-faint and hollow. He allows his eyes to close, and dreams of leaping in slow motion on the moon's surface, lunar dust compacted with each step. He imagines it would sound like snow crunching beneath his moon shoes. His body submits to the cool illicit pleasures of solitude.

Fly out. From the air, the mines look like bloody scabs. The dark grey frameworks of buildings glisten like fresh tattoos, ground into the raw inflamed skin of the land. This land was already red and sore and burnt before they even started digging. It's as though they are airing out buried ghosts, he thinks. His head stings at the top of the skull. His mind feels itchy and ant-ridden. He dips it into the promise that he will give up drinking this time, and it emerges quiet and absolved, ready for touch down.

Pamela Seckin

AMELIE

I want to be Amelie. Chop my hair off and put on a French accent howdy-do-da that's all there is to it. Maybe I could take it one step further, I could move to France. I've never left Sydney before and I don't speak any languages but that's okay because everything always works out in the end. I could see the Moulin Rouge of an evening, sip espresso in the morning and meet a handsome young man collecting photographs in front of the table where I sit. He would look up at me and exclaim his shock at seeing my beauty. He would comment on my haircut, so quirky so cute, and ask to meet me under the Eiffel Tower that afternoon. I would wait five minutes then realise he can't find me among all the tourists. I'd look for his face only to lose hope. I'd buy some kind of pastry and become a flâneur for the rest of the afternoon, walking with my dress flapping in the warm winds. I would drink everyone in, swallowing their hearts until they tell me their truths, then spit them out all moist and bewildered and I would be Amelie.

Tricia Dearborn

DANCING WITH THE MACHINE

One hand on your belly, turn your head to the right. It reminds you of the three lessons you had before you fell in love and your flamenco days were over. *There'll be four plates.* Don't bother smiling, your face is out of range. *Ok, now we'll get it from the other angle.* Lean your arm across your partner's cold metallic shoulder. *Can you take a little pressure? A little more?*

A new room and another partner. Just met her, already she's at second base. *It's real all right,* she says. You'd been hoping you wouldn't have to go all the way.

On the monitor, dark eels swim in a sea of static. The probe clicks along in its own jelly pool. You try to prepare yourself for the line of light that will pierce the pulsing greys. The needle enters at the point where you are marked with an X.

Good news: you get to sit the next one out.

Julie Chevalier

ROQUEFORT

He lifts a picnic kit from the Alfa Romeo Giulia Spider he's parked on the sandstone cliff overlooking the river. *In 1962, virgin bush as far as you could see. The marriage ceremony was right here,* he tells the woman smoothing creases from her mini skirt. She slips the narrow belt around until the buckle is centred. He spreads a damask cloth over the weathered table. From the picnic basket he takes a Thermos, a dusty Chateau Margaux, grapes in three colours. A rye loaf, a wedge of cheese. Blue veins on the wrinkled skin on the back of his hands, a vertical scar. He uses a linen napkin to rub a finger print off the throat of a wine glass. Unwraps two porcelain plates, smooth and unblemished as her forehead. He reaches for the corkscrew. She reaches for her iPhone.

Bella Li

A BIRTHMARK IN THE SHAPE OF PUGLIA

If Marjorie been born earlier, and somewhere besides Goolwa, she could have been a Hollywood star. Like Rita Hayworth. Long red hair – the right shade of red – long pale legs and, just beneath her right breast, a birthmark in the shape of Puglia. Marjorie wasn't sure where Puglia was, but an older man had said that to her once at the kiosk by the beach – a man with an impressive gold watch and well-groomed facial hair – and she'd thought it was a very astute remark. She liked the way it sounded: *pu-lee-yah*. She'd say it in front of the mirror every night, while brushing her long red hair, before she went to bed, and her brother would sometimes come in and say it too, to annoy her. And they'd both be staring at the mirror saying *pu-lee-yah, pu-lee-yah*, until she yelled at him and punched his arm. But not hard enough to ruin her nails.

Biographies

DAEL ALLISON writes poetry, essays and fiction and has received numerous literary awards. Poems from her book, *Fairweather's Raft*, featured in soundscape on ABC Poetica. She is a PhD student in Creative Writing at University Of Newcastle.

EVELYN ARALUEN is a PhD candidate and educator working with global Indigenous reading strategies at the University of Sydney. She is a founding member of grassroots activist network Students Support Aboriginal Communities, and speaks publically on a number of Aboriginal rights causes. Born and raised on Dharug land, she has ancestral and language ties to the Bundjalung nation. She was runner-up for the Nakata Brophy Prize for Young Indigenous Authors in 2016, and has been published in *Overland* and *Southerly*.

EMMA ASHMERE's short stories have appeared in *The Age*, *Review of Australian Fiction*, *Griffith Review*, *Text Journal*, and *Sleepers Almanac*. Her debut novel *The Floating Garden* (Spinifex Press) was shortlisted for the 2016 Most Underrated Book Award.

GAVIN AUSTIN's work has been published in many Australian journals and anthologies, been broadcast on Australian Community Radio, produced for several play festivals, and he has been successful in numerous writing competitions. Gavin's writing has also appeared in literary publications in NZ, the USA and the UK. He is currently putting together a collection of Japanese short form poetry.

DANIELLE BALDOCK has always lived in Sydney and has been writing as long as she can remember. She has a background in Science, and Childcare, but has always been writing in one form or another. She likes to write very short stories and poems, that capture a snapshot of time.

Originating in Sydney, with a childhood stint in West Bengal, **TENZIN BERENY** is now based in the sunny and sandy town of Hervey Bay. He is a Macquarie University graduate with a BA in English who looks forward to spending his existence traveling and creating. When Tenzin isn't writing he explores whatever is good in life, which he has mostly found to be edible.

AMANDA BERRY lives in the Upper Hunter valley (NSW) and works as a primary school teacher. She has a Masters degree in English Education and enjoys teaching, but dreams of being a travel writer. Amanda loves banksias, lemurs and drinking tea from fine china mugs.

JULIE CHEVALIER's third book, *Darger: his girls*, won the Alec Bolton Prize and was short-listed for the Western Australian Premier's Poetry Prize. Recently she co-edited *Cracking the Spine: ten Australian Short Stories and How They Were Written.*

SHADY COSGROVE is the author of *What the Ground Can't Hold* (Picador, 2013) and *She Played Elvis* (2009), which was shortlisted for the Australian Vogel Award. Her short fiction has appeared in *Best Australian Stories*, *Overland*, *Antipodes*, *Southerly* and other Spineless Wonders anthologies.

TRICIA DEARBORN has been widely published in numerous literary journals and anthologies including Contemporary Australian Poetry, Australian Poetry since 1788, The Best Australian Poems (2012 and 2010), and Australian Love Poems. She is on the editorial board of Plumwood Mountain, an online journal of ecopoetry and ecopoetics, and was poetry editor for the February 2016 edition. She has degrees in biochemistry and arts. Her most recent collection of poetry is The Ringing World (Puncher & Wattmann, 2012).

SUSI FOX is a writer and GP. She is currently working on her first manuscript for which she has received a Varuna Fellowship, a place on the QWC/Hachette Manuscript Development Program and a QWC/Olvar Wood Mentorship.

MAREE GALLOP is a Newcastle fiction writer and nurse with a Master of Mental Health Nursing. A finalist in the Hal Porter Short Story Competition 2014, her stories have been published in The Newcastle Herald and anthologies such as Grieve 2013 and Newcastle Short Story Award 2016 (HWC), Brio (Toowoomba Writers Festival Literary Prize and FAWQ 2015) and Award Winning Australian Writing 2016 (Melbourne Books).

TIM HEFFERNAN lives in the foothills of the Illawarra Escarpment in a village called Balgownie. He has been shortlisted for the joanne burns award in 2015 & 2016. As well as prose poetry and micro fiction Tim has an interest in Mad Poetry – he hosted a workshop and panel at the 2016 Wollongong Writers Festival.

PAUL HETHERINGTON is head of the International Poetry Studies Institute (IPSI) at the University of Canberra. He has published 11 poetry collections including *Burnt Umber* (UWAP, 2016) and won the 2014 Western Australian Premier's Book Awards (poetry).

HILARY HEWITT is a Sydney based writer. She has published poetry and short stories and was a runner up in the 2013 joanne burns Award for microfiction and prose poetry. She is currently writing a novel based on memories of growing up in Australia and France.

RICHARD HOLT is a visual artist and a writer of short stories and microfiction. His work has appeared in *Etchings*, *Visible Ink*, *Victorian Writer* and *Australian Love Poems* and been included in National Flash Fiction Day anthologies and previous Spineless Wonders anthologies. He was cofounder of Melbourne zine store, *Sticky* and produces microlit videos for outdoor screens under the banner 'Flashing the Square'. He blogs about microfiction at bigstorysmall.com.

MARJORIE LEWIS-JONES is a Sydney writer whose poetry and prose has been published by Spineless Wonders, ABC Radio National, Picaro Press, *Poetry Australia*, *Cordite*, Hunter Writers Centre, UTS, THRESHOLDS international short story forum, *Best Australian Writing 2015*, the ACU Prize for Poetry 2016, and in other anthologies. In 2014, she won the Carmel Bird Award and the Lane Cove Literary Award and her poetry has won awards in Australian competitions. She runs the literary blog, *A Bigger Brighter World*.

BELLA LI is a freelance editor and a managing co-editor at Five Islands Press. Her chapbook *Maps, Cargo* (Vagabond Press, 2013) was shortlisted for the Wesley Michel Wright Prize. Her first full-length book, *Argosy*, is forthcoming from Vagabond Press in 2017.

REBECCA LEHMAN is a short story writer who won the Reader's Digest 100 Word Story competition, was highly commended in the Langhorne Creek Writers' Festival, and was recently won the Katherine Susannah Pritchard Speculative Fiction Prize.

KAREN MANTON lives in Batchelor, Northern Territory. She has won NT Literary Awards several times and her short stories are published in *Bruno's Song*, *True North*, NT Literary Awards, *Award Winning Australian Writers*, *Review Australian Fiction*, NT *Writers Magazine* and *The Best Australian Stories*.

HARRIET MCINERNEY is a Sydney-based writer who works in book publishing. She is interested in the blurring of the real/ unreal, and has been published in places like *Mascara*, *Cordite* and *Voiceworks*.

SUSAN MIDALIA is a Perth-based author of three collections of short stories, all of them shortlisted for major literary awards: *A History of the Beanbag* (2007), *An Unknown Sky* (2102) and *Feet to the Stars* (2105). Her first novel will be published in early 2108 by Fremantle Press. She is currently on the board of writingWA and Margaret River Press.

MARK O'FLYNN has published five collections of poems. His novels include *Grassdogs*, and *The Forgotten World*. He has also published a collection of short fiction, *White Light*, (Spineless Wonders, 2013). His latest novel *The Last Days of Ava Langdon* is published by UQP, 2016.

TESS PEARSON is a Sydney-based writer of prose and poems. She holds a Master of Arts in Creative Writing, and has published short fiction in the UTS anthology *Hide Your Fires*, *Swamp*, *Short & Twisted*, and *Out of Place* (Spineless Wonders, 2015). Tess is working on a piece of long-form historical fiction set in Australia in the 1800s, and a research project on trauma and literature.

JENNIFER PORTER has written reviews for ArtsHub and has had work broadcast on Radio National. Her adult novel manuscript, *In Your Image*, has been listed for a number of national and international literary prizes. She also writes poetry, short stories and childrens' books. Jen is currently participating in the 2016 Hardcopy program and will travel to the Philippines to take part in the WrICE program in 2017.

LISA REILY is a former literacy consultant, dance director and teacher from Australia. She has had recent success in international competitions for screenwriting and short stories. Lisa recently set off for an indefinite period of travel and spends most of her time in Greece. Her website: lisareily.wordpress.com.

MARK ROBERTS is a Sydney based writer, critic and publisher. He is the founding editor of Rochford Street Review and editor of the occasional Lit Mag P76. His collection of poetry, *Concrete Flamingos*, was published by Island Press in February 2016.

RICHENDA RUDMAN has been a finalist in the Scarlett Stiletto Awards for short crime fiction and in 2014 won the Cross Genre prize. This year she won the People's Choice Poetry Award at Williamstown Literary Festival.

JEN SAUNDERS' work focuses on the local histories of her home - the South Coast of NSW. Her soundscapes, visual arts and writing draw on the intersections of Indigenous and colonial histories and particularly investigate concepts of naming, communication, memory and unseen inhabitants/traces in landscape. She was shortlisted in the 2017 Peter Porter Poetry Prize

SAMANTHA SEE is a twenty year old writer, theatre maker and university student who is based in Sydney. Her short story, 'Parental Rights', was published in the 2016 edition of ZineWest.

PAMELA SECKIN studied Creative Writing at the University of Wollongong. She enjoys the creative aspect that writing accommodates for, while also relishing the research process that writing entails. Pam will be undertaking further study to pursue a career as a librarian while continuing her writing.

BARNABY SMITH is based in northern New South Wales. His arts journalism has appeared in a variety of national and international titles, while he has published poetry in *Best Australian Poems*, *Southerly*, *Cordite*, FourW, *Otoliths*, *Writ* and more.

JANET THOMAS has a doctorate in Creative Writing from Flinders University. After a career in education she is now a full-time writer. Her blog, *Elixir: Creative and Reflexive Writing from the Third Age*, includes reflections on her PhD research, and on life in general, as well as a selection of her flash fiction.

ELIZABETH TYSON-DONELEY lives in tropical Brisbane and is a writer of poetry, plays and memoir. She has trained and worked in theatre and film production, as a performer, director, writer and production designer.

JODI VIAL is a former newspaper journalist and is currently enrolled as a third-year English major at The University of Newcastle. She lives with her husband, three daughters, one Labrador, two cats and six chickens in the outer suburbs of Newcastle and dreams about living closer to the sea.

SAMUEL WAGAN WATSON is a full time writer based in Brisbane. His last collection of poetry was awarded the Victorian Scanlon literary prize. 'Monsters Ink' is a recent body of work completed of 'experimental poetry' published by University of Canberra.

PATRICK WEST is a Senior Lecturer in Writing and Literature in the School of Communication and Creative Arts, Deakin University, Melbourne Campus. He has a PhD from The University of Melbourne on the feminist psychoanalysis of Julia Kristeva and he is a widely published creative writer primarily in the short story form. His current major research interest is in the relation-ships of architecture and writing.

CHLOE WILSON is the author of two poetry collections, *The Mermaid Problem* and *Not Fox Nor Axe*, which was shortlisted for the Kenneth Slessor Prize for Poetry and the Judith Wright Calanthe Award. She received equal first prize in the 2016 Josephine Ulrick Poetry Prize, and has been awarded the John Marsden Prize for Young Australian Writers, the (Melbourne) Lord

Mayor´s Creative Writing Award for Poetry, the Gwen Harwood Poetry Prize, the Fish Publishing Flash Fiction Prize and the Arts Queensland Val Vallis Award.

DANIELLE WOOD is an award-winning author whose books include *The Alphabet of Light and Dark*, *Rosie Little's Cautionary Tales for Girls* and *Mothers Grimm*. Along with Heather Rose, she is 'Angelica Banks', author of the internationally acclaimed Tuesday McGillycuddy trilogy for children. Danielle teaches writing at the University of Tasmania.

Editor

CASSANDRA ATHERTON is an award-winning writer, academic and critic. She is currently a Harvard Visiting Scholar in English. Her most recent books of prose poetry are *Trace* (Finlay Lloyd, 2015) and *Exhumed* (Grand Parade, 2015).

The joanne burns Award

Each year Spineless Wonders auspices an award for the best writing in the forms of prose poem and microfiction in honour of foremost Australian experimental poet, joanne burns. The award is open to people residing in Australia and to Australians living overseas. Finalists chosen by each year's judging panel are offered publication in our annual anthology alongside invited writers.

The inaugural *joanne burns Award* was held in 2011 and was judged by joanne burns who selected Charles D'Anastasi's 'Madame Bovary' as the winning entry and commended Erin Gough's 'William Shatner vows to save the Great Basin Pocket Mouse' and Clare McHugh's 'Briefly'. All three pieces, along with those of other finalists appear in *small wonder*, edited by Linda Godfrey and Julie Chevalier.

The *2012 joanne burns Award* was judged by Carol Jenkins who selected Mark O'Flynn's 'under the maw of luna park' as the winning entry and commended Richard Holt's 'bush burial', Trina Denner's 'playing outside', Stu Hatton's 'down south' and Paul Mitchell's 'The Old Man and the Pool'. The winner and finalists all appear in *Stoned Crows & other Australian Icons*, edited by Julie Chevalier and Linda Godfrey.

The *2013 joanne burns Award* was judged by Shady Cosgrove who selected Mark Smith's '10.42 to Sydenham' as the winning entry and Hilary Hewitt's 'happy' and Mark Robert's 'cities that are not Dublin' as runners-up. All three pieces, along with those of other finalists appear in *Writing to the Edge*, edited by Linda Godfrey and Ali Jane Smith.

In *2014, The joanne burns Award* was judged by Angela Meyer and Richard Holt who selected Susan McCreery's 'Hold Up' as the winning entry and Kirsten Tranter's 'Turing Test Study Guide' and Mark Smith's 'The Meteorologist's Daughter' as runners up. All three pieces, along with those of other finalists are published in *Flashing the Square*, edited by Linda Godfrey and Bronwyn Mehan.

The 2015 joanne burns Award was judged by Kirsten Tranter who selected Nick Couldwell's 'Dancing' as the winning entry. Runners up were Tim Heffernan for 'Butterflies in Iraq' and Matthew Gabriel for 'jesussaves82'. All three pieces, along with those of other finalists and invited contributors are published in *Out of Place* edited by Kirsten Tranter and Linda Godfrey.

The 2016 joanne burns Microlit Award was co-sponsored by the Newcastle Writers Festival. The national category, judged by Cassandra Atherton, was won by Tim Heffernan for 'Barunga Conversation' and the Newcastle category, judged by Karen Whitelaw and Joanna Atherfold Finn, was won by Dael Allison for 'Breakwall'. The winning entries and finalists from both categories as well as invited contributors are published in *Landmarks* edited by Cassandra Atherton.

About joanne burns

joanne burns grew up in Sydney's eastern suburbs. She worked as an English teacher in New South Wales, and for a time in London. She has taught creative writing in tertiary institutions, schools and community organisations. Her first collection of poems, *Snatch*, was published in London in 1972. Since then she has published more than a dozen further books of poetry. Her poems have appeared in numerous Australian literary journals, poetry magazines and have been set for study on the Higher School Certificate syllabus. joanne has been particularly concerned with the blurring of the distinctions between poetry and prose in her work, and has written extensively in prose poem/ microfiction forms. She has also written monologues and short futurist fictions and 'farables' (fables/ parables).Her latest collection *Brush* was published by Giramondo Poets in 2014. In 2016, she was awarded the New South Wales Premiers' Kenneth Slessor Literary Award for Poetry.

Spineless Wonders publications are available in print, digital and audio format from participating bookshops and online. For further information, go to the Spineless Wonders website:

www.shortaustralianstories.com.au

More microlit from
SPINELESS WONDERS

Small Wonder
prose poems & microfiction

edited by Linda Godfrey and Julie Chevalier

Here are short and clever pieces by thirty contemporary Australian writers on the eroticism of mashed potato, parenting as magic realism and a tongue-in-cheek history of the Cyclops bicycle. Includes award-winning writers Michael Farrell, Keri Glastonbury, Judith Beveridge and Peter Boyle. Features prose poems and microfiction selected by competition judge joanne burns.

Illustrated by talented young artist, Paden Hunter.

Stoned Crows
& other Australian Icons
prose poems & microfiction

edited by Linda Godfrey and Julie Chevalier

What do our best wordsmiths have to say about Australian icons? This anthology takes a fresh look at everything from the HIH collapse to crocs, Margaret Olley, bush burials and the ABC. We visit a post-apocalyptic Opera House and spend Saturday night in downtown Byron Bay. Tones range from nostalgic to sceptical, from wry to LOL. Featuring prose poems and microfiction by Mark O'Flynn, Anna Kerdijk Nicholson, Michael Sharkey, Moya Costello and many more.

Writing to the Edge
prose poems & microfiction
edited by Linda Godfrey and Ali Jane Smith

Flashing The Square
edited by Linda Godfrey & Bronwyn Mehan

This collection takes its name from an event at the Melbourne Writers Festival, where these miniature vignettes and mini-narratives were flashed on screens in Federation Square. There's a high standard of writing here across a broad range of subjects.The best contributions are full of potential and feeling: Susan McCreery's one-paragraph sketch of a service-station hold-up fills the reader with dread, and Michelle Wright's *Taken*, about a shark attack, with a kind of difficult grief. Ally Scale's *I Do* is heartbreaking and Shady Cosgrove's *Call an Ambulance* quite terrifying; for some reason the stories about unreasoning violence work best. Other contributors include such familiar names as Kirsten Tranter and A.S. Patric, as well as Angela Meyer.

Kerry Goldsworthy, SYDNEY MORNING HERALD

Out of Place

edited by Kirsten Tranter & Linda Godfrey

In Spineless Wonders' latest anthology, Australia's best micro-wordsmiths have produced writing which reflects on dislocation — in space, time, feeling, psyche and memory.
Here are big stories rendered in miniature and fleeting moments captured with elaborate focus.

'With the unsettling perfection of the miniature, this is a collection of sparkling treasures - each one demanding to be held up examined, re-examined and then marvelled over.'

GEORGIA BLAIN

9 781925 052312